PUPPY PATROL ™

THE SNOW DOG

BOOKS IN THE PUPPY PATROL™ SERIES

COMING SOON

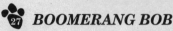

PUPPY PATROL ™

THE SNOW DOG

JENNY DALE

Illustrations by Mick Reid
Cover illustration by Michael Rowe

AN
APPLE
PAPERBACK

SCHOLASTIC INC.
New York Toronto London Auckland Sydney
Mexico City New Delhi Hong Kong Buenos Aires

SPECIAL THANKS TO CHERITH BALDRY

No part of this publication may be reproduced, in whole or in part, or stored in a
retrieval system, or transmitted in any form or by any means, electronic,
mechanical, photocopying, recording, or otherwise, without written permission
of the publisher. For information regarding permission,
write to Macmillan Publishers Ltd., 20 New Wharf Rd.,
London N1 9RR Basingstoke and Oxford.

ISBN 0-439-45347-X

Text copyright © 1999 by Working Partners Limited.
Illustrations copyright © 1999 by Mick Reid.

All rights reserved. Published by Scholastic Inc., 557 Broadway,
New York, NY 10012 by arrangement with Macmillan Children's Books,
a division of Macmillan Publishers Ltd.

SCHOLASTIC and associated logos are trademarks and/or registered trademarks
of Scholastic Inc.

12 11 10 9 8 7 6 5 4 3   5 6 7 8/0

Printed in the U.S.A.   40
First Scholastic printing, May 2003

CHAPTER ONE

Neil Parker stamped his feet to keep them warm and pulled his cap farther down over his spiky brown hair. The fresh wintry air felt bitterly cold compared to the warm train car he had left a few minutes ago.

"Where's Penny?" he asked. "She said she'd be here to meet us."

He was standing with his sister Emily in the station's parking lot at Beckthwaite in the Lake District. Jake, his young black-and-white Border collie, barked and danced around, winding his leash around Neil's legs. He was a healthy and active dog, not much more than a puppy, with glossy fur and bright eyes.

"Chill out, you goofy dog," said Neil, laughing. Jake looked up at him, his jaws wide open as if he were laughing, too.

"Wow, it's cold!" said Emily, beginning to shiver. "Much colder than at home."

Eleven-year-old Neil and his younger sister Emily lived in the small country town of Compton, where their parents ran King Street Kennels, a boarding kennel and rescue center. The Parkers were so committed to dogs that their friends called them the Puppy Patrol.

Back in Compton there wasn't any snow, but here it lay thick on the station roof, and long icicles hung from the gutters. Behind the station, the hills were giant white mounds against a gray sky.

"I hope Penny likes the Christmas present I bought her," said Emily. "It's a book about —"

"There she is!" Neil interrupted, pointing at a large Range Rover that was turning into the station's parking lot. As the car pulled up beside Neil and Emily, Penny Ainsworth scrambled out of the backseat with her magnificent Great Dane, King. Her face was pink with cold but she was smiling broadly.

"Hi, Penny," said Neil. "How's King these days?" He ruffled the big dog's fur.

Neil and Emily had first met Penny when they spent a week camping near Beckthwaite. King had been suffering from a serious eye condition that threatened his vision. It was mainly due to Neil that

King had been able to have the operation he badly needed.

"King's fine," said Penny. "See for yourself!"

King was a huge dog with a honey-colored coat, broad chest, and strong legs. Neil bent over, took King's head in both hands, and peered at him. King accepted the examination calmly, looking back at Neil with eyes that were clear and undamaged.

"You're looking really well, aren't you, boy?" Neil held out one of the dog treats he always carried in his pocket. As King lowered his head to take it, Jake

pushed his nose in, demanding his share of the tidbits.

"This must be Jake," Penny said, ruffling the fur under his chin. "I've been looking forward to meeting him." Suddenly serious, she added, "Neil, I was sorry to hear about Sam."

Neil straightened up. "Yeah, well . . ."

He still found it hard to talk about Sam, Jake's dad and Neil's best friend. The Border collie had died heroically a few months before, and Neil hadn't stopped missing him. This would be Neil's first Christmas without Sam, and he wasn't looking forward to it.

"How's the film going?" Emily asked. Neil guessed she was tactfully trying to change the subject.

Penny's face lit up with enthusiasm. "It's very exciting! Max and Prince are great."

The film was why Neil and Emily were visiting Ainsworth Castle so close to Christmas. Their friend Max Hooper and his dog Prince were the stars of their favorite TV show, *The Time Travelers*. On their previous visit, he had been looking for a castle to use as Camelot in a feature film about King Arthur. Ainsworth Castle was perfect. Although Penny's dad, Lord Ainsworth, had needed some persuading before he would allow the company to film there, he eventually saw the sense in it. The fee had paid for King's operation and helped with the Ainsworths' other money problems.

While they were talking, Lord Ainsworth had gotten out of the car. He was a tall man with a bristling mustache and a shapeless tweed hat rammed down over his ears.

He held out a hand to shake. "Neil and Emily. Welcome back."

"Thank you," said Emily. She always felt as if Penny's dad expected her to call him *sir*.

Lord Ainsworth heaved the Parkers' luggage into the car's trunk. "All aboard!" he said cheerfully.

"Do you mind if we walk?" Neil asked. "Jake hasn't had any exercise yet today, and he's been stuck on the train for hours."

"Whatever you like," said Ainsworth.

He drove off, leaving Neil and the others to walk along the road which led from the station through the center of the village. All the shops were bright with holiday decorations, and nearly every house had a Christmas tree in the window. The faint sound of Christmas carols drifted out from one of the shops and gave them all a warm holiday feeling as they trudged along.

"Thanks for letting us stay, Penny," said Neil. "I've really been looking forward to this break." It would be five days before he and Emily went home on Christmas Eve.

"No problem," replied Penny.

"The film sounds great. Are you going to be in it, too?" Emily asked. Neil and Emily were scheduled to have brief walk-on parts.

"Yes. I'm one of Queen Guinevere's ladies. I have to sit in the background and sew a lot." Penny made a face. "A lot of the locals are extras, too."

At the other end of the village, a narrow lane led down to Ainsworth Castle. Snowplows had heaped snow so high on both sides that Neil felt like he was walking through a white tunnel. Jake scrabbled excitedly at the frozen walls, but King paced alongside Penny with a more dignified air.

"Doesn't all this snow spoil the filming?" asked Emily as her boots crunched underfoot.

"No, the film is *meant* to be set in winter." Penny's eyes shined. "It's so exciting! They've built a whole village in the clearing beside the lake."

"Cool!" said Neil.

Jake barked his agreement.

Soon they reached Ainsworth Castle, which was built on an island in the lake itself. It was joined to the shore by a short stone bridge leading to an arched gate with an overhanging iron grate. Gray towers rose up behind thick walls and scarlet pennants fluttered from the battlements. There couldn't be any better place, Neil thought, to be King Arthur's legendary castle at Camelot.

"Max said to go straight down to the village," said Penny. "I won't come with you. I promised to help wrap Christmas presents."

"Sure," said Neil. "See you later, then."

Penny started across the stone bridge with King.

The footpath to the set led off to the right through the woods around the lakeshore. By now Jake had run off some of his energy, and was trotting at Neil's heel, only now and then darting away to snuffle in the hollows under the trees.

There were deep ruts in the snow where heavy vehicles had passed, and busy footprints in both directions. Neil and Emily plodded through the slush until they came to the edge of the trees.

Here Neil stopped and pursed his lips in a soundless whistle. "Wow! Just look at that!"

Ahead of them stood a medieval village. Small huts built of wood and interlaced branches were grouped around a central square flanked by bigger buildings. One of them had a sign saying it was an inn. Neil and Emily could see that the buildings weren't real, just front and side walls, all held up at the back with wooden supports and metal scaffolding poles.

On one side of the village were parked several modern trailers, with a group of people in medieval costume standing around drinking tea from plastic cups. On the other side, two or three horses with brightly colored coverings stood calmly beside their handlers. A knight was mounted on one of them, wearing silver armor and a white cloak with red diagonal stripes. Film cameras were positioned all around the village, focused on the central area.

As Neil and Emily watched, they heard a sudden

outburst of barking and a golden cocker spaniel came racing into the village square from behind the inn, his silky ears flying and his long, feathery tail flowing out behind him.

"It's Prince!" said Emily.

Neil bent over, clipped a leash on Jake's collar, and put a hand on the young dog's muzzle to quiet him — just in case he ruined the scene by barking in reply.

As Prince dashed across the square, Max appeared in costume as Zeno, his character in *The Time Travelers*. He was running after Prince, only to slip and fall facedown in the snow. Behind him, a knight in black armor appeared on a magnificent black horse and hurtled toward him, bending low in the saddle as if he was going to slash Max with his sword.

"Oh, no!" Emily whispered. "He'll kill Max!"

As she spoke, a voice yelled "Cut!" and another man strode out into the square. He was youngish, with blond hair, and was wearing a thick sheepskin jacket with its collar turned up.

"That's Brian Mason," Neil said, recognizing the director of *The Time Travelers*. "What's eating him? The scene looked all right to me."

"Where's Sir Lancelot?" shouted the director.

Max got up and brushed the snow off himself.

Another mounted knight, the one in silver armor, urged his horse forward a few paces into the square.

He flicked up his visor. The actor was young and dark-haired, with a bad-tempered expression.

Emily nudged Neil. "That's Brett Benson," she said. "He's Sir Lancelot in the film. He's gorgeous!"

"I'm sorry I missed my cue," Brett Benson said. "But it was this wretched dog — he got in the way of the horse."

"That's not fair!" Neil said hotly. "Prince was nowhere near his horse!" Neil could not help himself — he had to make sure the director didn't blame Prince for something he didn't do. With Jake in tow he marched across to Brian Mason and the knight, and bent to rumple Prince's ears as the cocker spaniel bounded up, barking excitedly. "Sorry to interrupt, Mr. Mason," he said. "I was watching just now and thought Prince was fine." Neil glared up at the mounted knight.

Brett Benson glared back. "Huh! How am I supposed to work when the set's swarming with kids? Where's the dog trainer?"

"Here." The woman who spoke was tall and blond, wearing a red down jacket. "And this 'kid' is quite right, Brett. Prince *wasn't* in the way."

Brian Mason gave Neil a distracted look. "Oh, hello, Neil." He quickly turned away. "It doesn't matter. Let's go again. Maggie, make sure you hang on to Prince when he runs over here, OK? All right, folks, places everybody . . . come on, hurry. Brett, you're going to be great."

Brett gave Neil another dirty look, and adjusted his helmet. Max came up, tossed off a "hi, talk to you in a minute," and went off again with Prince.

Two members of the film crew hurried to the set from the trailers to check that the actors' costumes and makeup were ready for the new take.

The blond woman smiled at Neil and Emily and said, "You must be the Parkers. I'm Maggie Brown, the film's dog trainer. From what Max has told me, it sounds as if you're just as into dogs as I am!"

Before Neil and Emily could say hello, the barking

began again. This time, when Prince dashed across the square, Maggie was waiting to grip him by the collar.

The scene went according to plan, and when Max was out of range of the cameras, he relaxed and walked over to join Neil and the others with the dogs. "Thanks for sticking up for Prince. Brett Benson's a real pain."

Emily looked disappointed. "I thought he'd be nice."

"No way." Max sounded angry. "He can't stand it that Prince is the real star of this film. He complains the whole time."

Max squatted down to pat Prince, and the dog licked his face enthusiastically. "You were great, boy," he said, admiring his shining golden coat and his lively, intelligent expression. "By the way, it's great to see you both — and Jake," he added quickly, as the young collie pushed forward, demanding attention. "And I've got news for you . . ."

"What is it?" Emily asked excitedly.

"Something really special." Max sounded mysterious. "But you have to wait until we get back to the castle." He called to the director as he came striding up. "Brian, are we finished?"

"No, sorry," Brian said. "Before the daylight goes, I want to pick up the scene where you're searching for Sir Kay."

"OK," said Max. He turned to Neil and Emily. "This shouldn't take long. It's just me and Prince."

"Right," said Brian, leading Max back toward the square. Neil and the others followed and waited at the edge of the acting area, where they overheard the director reminding Max of the scene. "Sir Kay went to fight the Black Knight and was captured. You and Prince look for him, and Prince finds him wounded inside the inn. He barks to you out of the window, and you go in. Have you got that?"

Max nodded.

"We'll rehearse it once," said Brian, "and then we'll go for a take."

Maggie strode across the village square and into the inn, ready to make sure that Prince barked on cue. Max and Prince both vanished around a corner.

Moments later, the crew settled down and Brian called, "Action!"

Prince reappeared, sniffing his way across the square until he pawed at the inn door. It swung open, and Prince went in. Now Zeno came cautiously out of the opposite doorway, peered through the window of the next house, and moved on.

A camera running alongside him on tracks followed his progress.

The shutters of one of the inn windows were pushed open. Prince had his front paws up on the sill and let out a sharp bark. Zeno looked up. Then, as Prince barked again, the sound was drowned out by a sudden crash and a splintering noise as the roof of the inn sagged inward.

Max yelled, "Prince!" and started to run.

Prince scrabbled at the sill as if he was trying to climb out. Then he vanished as the walls started to tilt crazily like a collapsing house of cards.

"It's falling apart!" Neil exclaimed from his vantage point nearby. "Prince will be trapped!"

CHAPTER TWO

Without a moment's hesitation, Neil thrust Jake's leash into Emily's hands and sprinted across the square toward the collapsing building. Max ducked his head and vanished inside. Neil followed, even though he heard Brian Mason yelling, "No! Come back!"

Inside, the air was thick with dust. Blinking because it stung his eyes, Neil saw that some of the scaffolding poles had collapsed and Max was trying to climb over them.

"Prince is here somewhere," he gasped when he saw Neil. "But I can't see him. Or Maggie."

Neil couldn't see them, either. In the far corner was a wooden staircase leading up to the window where Prince had appeared. It looked as if some of the steps had given way and pulled the outer wall down with them. The scaffolding had shifted so that it wasn't holding up the roof properly. The roof was tilted inward, half covering the remains of the stairs.

Neil thought Prince and Maggie had to be somewhere underneath. He could still hear Brian yelling at him from outside, but he paid no attention. Scrambling over the scaffolding poles, he reached the sagging roof.

"Max — help me shift this!" he yelled, coughing as the dust got into his throat.

There was a sudden whining from beneath the board, and then Maggie Brown's voice. "I've got Prince. We're OK, I think . . ."

With Max beside him, Neil grabbed the edge of the board and heaved upward. For a few seconds it refused to budge.

"It's caught on something," Max said, trying to get his shoulder underneath.

Neil and Max hauled on the roof again. Suddenly, Neil realized there was someone else beside them, helping to lift the weight. The roof swung upward, and Maggie Brown, almost doubled over, stumbled out, pushing Prince in front of her.

The man beside Neil let go of the roof, grabbed Prince by the collar, and dragged him through the gap at the back of the building. Maggie followed him as Neil and Max let the roof drop. Neil staggered, off-balance, as it crashed down, and wrapped his arms around his head to protect himself from a rain of debris.

Just as Neil clutched Max's arm and pulled his friend to safety, he heard a soft crunching sound, and behind him the whole of the village inn folded and settled into a heap of wreckage.

Maggie Brown was kneeling on the ground outside, trying to get her breath. The other man was still holding Prince. Weak with relief, Neil staggered toward them. "Thanks!" he gasped. "That was great! Are you all right?"

The man let Prince go and straightened up. He had thinning dark hair and a straggly beard, and he wore the drab tunic and leggings of a medieval peasant. His face was smeared with makeup and dust.

"No problem," he said abruptly. "I think the dog's OK."

Before Neil could reply, Emily came dashing up, along with Jake and a tall, dark-haired young woman. Neil recognized Suzie, Max's chaperone, who had to be on set when he was filming. Right now she looked furious.

"Do you know what might have happened?" she said to Neil. "You and Max could have been killed!"

"We had to save Prince," Max said, falling to his knees beside his beloved dog and running his hands over him to check for injuries. "Thanks, Neil, you were great."

"It wasn't me," Neil started to explain. "It was . . ." He looked around, but the peasant had disappeared. "Hey, where did he go?"

"I didn't see him leave — but I'm so grateful to him. Maybe he was one of the extras," said Max. "Tell me if you see him, Neil. I want to thank him. I don't think Prince is hurt at all."

"What happened?" Emily asked. "What made it collapse like that?"

By now Maggie had recovered, and was helping Max to examine Prince. "I don't know," she said. "I was waiting inside, ready for Prince to come down from the window. When I put my weight on the steps they gave way, and then the whole place started to come down."

"Are you all right, Maggie?" asked Brian Mason,

approaching and peering at Prince over Max's shoulder.

"Bruised, that's all," said Maggie with a smile. "It's Prince I'm worried about."

Prince was standing quietly. The shock had subdued his usual boisterous nature. Neil guessed that would soon wear off, and the cocker spaniel didn't seem to be physically injured.

"We'd better get the vet to check him out," said Brian. "Go up to the castle and give him a call." He gestured toward the ruins of the inn. "Now we'll be held up again until this is fixed. Honestly, sometimes I think there's a jinx on this film."

Neil and the others headed for the castle. Flakes of snow started to drift down and quickly grew into thick flurries that were swept across the path by the wind. Neil hunched his shoulders and buried his hands deep in his pockets.

"Max," he asked, "what did Brian mean — about a jinx on the film?"

Max frowned, looking worried. "This isn't the first accident," he said. "A couple of days ago, one of the horses went berserk when he had a scene with Prince. Prince was nearly trampled, weren't you, boy? And then, on another day, part of my costume went missing and turned up in Prince's basket! Brian thought he'd dragged it in there, but I know he didn't."

"Prince would never do anything like that," said Emily.

Daylight was beginning to fade as they reached the open space in front of Ainsworth Castle. The snow shined eerily in the dying light. Neil tramped thankfully across the stone bridge, looking forward to a hot drink and something to eat.

The arched gateway led into a courtyard. The main entrance to the castle was opposite at the top of a flight of steps, through a pair of thick wooden doors studded with iron nails. Neil and the others stood stamping snow off their boots in the hallway, while Jake shook himself and showered everybody with icy drops. Maggie disappeared, saying she would phone the vet.

"Max, you told us you had some news," Emily said.

"Yeah," said Neil, stripping off his jacket. "And that we had to wait for it until we got back to the castle. So come on, what is it?"

Max started to smile, his worried look vanishing. "You'll really like this," he promised. "Won't they, Prince?"

Prince barked in agreement.

"I'll have to find Adrian," Max went on. "He said he'd help while I'm on set."

Max pulled open the doors to the Great Hall and went inside. Neil followed him, giving Emily a puzzled look, wondering what Adrian Bartlett, Lord

Ainsworth's steward, had to do with Max's secret. Then he stood still, gaping. "Wow!" he exclaimed.

Neil had been in the hall of Ainsworth Castle before, but he had never seen it like this. Tapestries covered the walls. Iron sconces holding torches were fixed to the pillars. Over the enormous fireplace at the far end, brightly painted shields were hanging. A huge round table stood in the middle, surrounded by carved wooden seats.

"King Arthur's Great Hall," Max said.

Neil could easily imagine armored knights coming to sit in council around the table. It took him a minute to notice the lights fixed high in the roof, and remember that this was a film set.

"It's wonderful!" said Emily. "It looks so authentic!"

In front of the fireplace were two people Neil recognized: Jeff Calton, the producer of *The Time Travelers,* and Adrian Bartlett. Adrian was a smallish man with blond hair and a thin, beaky face. He broke off what he was saying to Jeff as Neil and the others came in.

"Hello," he said, smiling. "Welcome to Camelot."

"Adrian," said Max, "where's . . . you know?"

Adrian's eyes twinkled. "Over here."

He beckoned them toward King Arthur's Round Table, and the massive carved chair where the king himself would sit. As Neil came closer, he saw a tiny head looking up from the chair's velvet cushion. A

silky golden head, with soft, floppy ears and huge brown eyes. One silky paw was dangling over the edge. The little pup stirred and let out a high-pitched yap.

Prince went to stand beside the chair, and looked up at the miniature of himself, whining softly.

Max's grin was wide enough to split his face. "Meet Princess," he said.

CHAPTER THREE

"**O**h, she's gorgeous!" Emily exclaimed. "Can I hold her?"

Max carefully lifted the cocker spaniel pup, and Emily cuddled her with a blissful smile on her face.

"Where did you get her?" Neil asked. "And why didn't you tell us?"

"She's Prince's daughter," Max said. He looked a bit embarrassed. "We were on vacation this summer in a cottage in Wales, and some people down the road had a female cocker spaniel called Merry. She and Prince got together before anybody knew about it."

Emily giggled. "Prince, you naughty dog!"

"They were all good pups," Max went on, "and Merry's owner was pleased in the end. I didn't tell you before, because I wasn't sure if I could have

Princess. I've only just gotten her — she's my Christmas present from Mom and Dad."

"She's a *great* present," said Emily. She held Princess close and stroked her head. "You're going to be a star just like your dad!"

Princess gave a sharp little yap as if she agreed, and swiped her tongue over Emily's face.

"She's a star already," said Max.

"What are you feeding her?" Neil asked.

"I wanted to ask you about that," Max said. "Merry's owner recommended the puppy meal that she uses, but it looks a bit boring to me. What can I give Princess to make her meals more interesting?"

"You need the Puppy Patrol advice service, pal," Neil said. He always had all the latest dog-care facts at his fingertips. "How old is she?"

"Twelve weeks."

"Well, when Jake was a young pup I used to give him cereal and milk for variety. Then you could start adding in just a little bit of meat, with some rice, or maybe pasta —"

"Hey, I'm not running a restaurant!" said Max, laughing.

Jake tentatively approached the chair and sniffed the young spaniel pup. Princess drew back initially, then yapped and welcomed the Border collie to her castle with a brief touching of their black button noses.

Everybody laughed.

"Plenty of fresh drinking water, too," Neil went on, "but you know that anyway. And not too many treats, because —"

Before he could finish, Jeff Calton, who had been scribbling notes on a clipboard, came up and said, "What's the matter? You two are filthy! And Prince!"

Max explained about the collapsing village inn, and how he and Neil had rescued Prince. "Maggie's gone to phone the vet to get him to check Prince out," he finished.

As Max was speaking, Jeff had begun to look more and more angry. "I've had enough of this!" he said. "The film can't stand further delays. Now I'll have to talk to Brian and get those scenes rescheduled. I'll have a few words to say to the set builders, too."

He strode off. Then Adrian said, "I'd better let Lord Ainsworth know as well," and followed him.

Max was starting to look worried again. Hoping to take his friend's mind off his problems, Neil asked, "So what's this film all about?"

"Well," Max explained, "Zeno and Prince get carried back through the time tunnel to the court of King Arthur. They meet the witch queen Morgan le Fay, and she steals the time tunnel controller, so Zeno can't get away. Morgan wants to kill King Arthur and make herself High Queen, so Zeno and Prince help Arthur to defeat her."

"Sounds great," Neil said.

"But just a minute," Emily objected. "King Arthur's

a legend. He wasn't real, was he? I mean, not like this, with a castle and knights and a Round Table. So how can Zeno get into his time?"

Max shrugged and grinned. "Don't ask me, ask the scriptwriters!"

While Max changed out of his costume, Neil and Emily phoned their mom and dad to tell them they'd arrived safely. Carole Parker answered the phone.

"How was your trip?" she asked when Emily had poured out all the news about Princess. "The TV news said there was snow up there."

"Lots of it!" said Neil. "Listen, Mom, there's something I forgot to say. Keep Squirt out of my bedroom, will you? I've hidden all your Christmas presents in there."

"*Sarah* is teaching Fudge to sing 'Jingle Bells.' I think that will keep her occupied over the next few days."

Neil laughed. His little sister, Sarah, thought that Fudge, her hamster, was clever enough to do anything. "That's just like Squirt!" he said, still laughing as he said good-bye and put the phone down.

Neil woke the next morning to find that Jake had jumped up onto his bed and started to lick his face. "Get off, troublemaker!" he said, pushing Jake gently to one side and sitting up.

The bedroom was cold and dark — Ainsworth

Castle had no central heating — and when Neil squinted at the clock on the bedside table he saw that it was still only seven. He would have liked to crawl back under the warm blankets and sleep for another hour, but as soon as Jake saw that he had succeeded in waking up his owner, the young dog leaped off the bed and started to paw at the door.

"OK, boy," Neil said, sighing heavily. "You win! Walk before breakfast."

He took a quick shower and pulled on warm clothes and boots. Before he had finished getting ready, his door burst open and Emily came in.

"There was more snow overnight," she said excitedly. "D'you think the road to the village will be blocked? We might be cut off!"

Neil stifled a yawn. "I don't think so. Coming for a walk?"

With Jake pattering behind, they went down the back staircase and along the passage past the kitchen which led into the courtyard. Even here they could see how the film crew had taken over the castle. Lighting equipment was stacked in a storeroom just inside the side door, and across the passage the old castle scullery had been transformed into a makeup room, with stage makeup strewn over tables and lines of chairs facing mirrors propped against the wall.

A girl was there, touching up the makeup of one of the cast members. Neil caught a glimpse of the man's face in the mirror as he walked past. It was the extra who had helped save Prince when the set collapsed the day before. The girl was loading some filthy gunk onto his face.

"Hello," Neil said, stopping in the doorway. "Wasn't it you who —"

The makeup girl jumped at the sound of his voice. "Do you mind?" she said irritably. "There are people here trying to concentrate."

She flounced across the room and slammed the door in Neil's face.

Neil gaped. "What did I say?"

"You startled her," Emily said. "Maybe she just doesn't like people watching her work."

Neil shrugged. He'd only wanted to thank the man for helping Prince. Still, he told himself, maybe anybody would be feeling snappy if they had to start work at this time in the morning.

He followed Emily into the courtyard, where they met Max with Prince, and Princess tucked into the front of his padded jacket.

"I thought we'd be the first ones up," said Neil.

Max laughed and shook his head. "Not on a film set! Every day's an early start."

"Yes," said Emily. "There's someone in makeup already."

"They'll want me soon," said Max, "but I've got just enough time to walk Prince."

Together they crossed the stone bridge and took the footpath that led to the lake.

Where the path curved down to the water's edge, more early risers had gathered. Neil didn't recognize some of them, but he assumed they were actors in the film. Looking out across the lake, he saw Penny, with Adrian Bartlett, skimming along expertly on ice skates. She raised a hand to wave as she glided past.

"I'd liked to do that," Emily said. "Do you think Penny would teach me?"

"I suppose so," said Neil. "Better be careful, though."

"The ice is safe enough for now," Lord Ainsworth said. He was standing beside the lake with King, watching the skaters. "I tested it myself, first thing."

Even so, Neil wasn't too sure about ice skating. He carried on around the lake with Emily and Max while Jake and Prince played together, chasing each other and plunging through the fresh, powdery snow. Prince was his usual lively self. Max reported that the vet from Beckthwaite, David Blackburn, had checked him over the night before and found no injury from his accident.

"Neil," Max said, "do you think it's OK to let Princess run around? It won't be too cold for her in all this snow?"

"Well, she can't stay inside your jacket all day," Neil said, laughing. "She'll be fine if you don't keep her out for too long. And make sure you give her a good toweling off when we get back."

Max put the wriggling Princess down in the snow. She sniffed at it and sneezed, and then took off after her dad and Jake, her feathery tail waving and her long ears bouncing up and down. Excited little yaps came from her as she ran.

Neil shook his head. "You've got your work cut out there!"

Farther along the lake, Neil caught sight of Maggie Brown walking back toward the castle with an enormous dog at her side. He grabbed Emily's arm. "Hey, there's Fred!"

As he spoke, the dog gave a welcoming bark and began loping ahead of the trainer. He was huge, with a rough gray coat and a long tail which waved enthusiastically as he came up to Neil. Neil rumpled his ears and fished in his pocket for a dog treat. "Hi, Fred," he said. "What's it like being a movie star?"

Fred was an Irish wolfhound who had taken part in the *Time Travelers* episode filmed at Padsham Castle near Neil's home at King Street Kennels.

He'd been such a hit as another heroic knight's war hound that Jeff Calton had asked for him again, to play the part of King Arthur's favorite hound, Cabal.

"He loves it," Maggie said as she caught up. "Bill had to go home, but Fred doesn't seem to be missing him too much."

Bill Gray, Fred's owner, ran a butcher's shop in Padsham, and the few days before Christmas were the busiest of the year for him.

"If you like, I'll help —" Neil began, and then broke off. Out of the corner of his eye he had seen Jake dash out onto the frozen lake. Neil spun around to see him darting in and out of the group of skaters, with Prince on his heels, barking madly, and Princess doing her best to keep up.

Max laughed as Brett Benson tripped over Prince and only just managed to right himself and avoid falling flat on his back.

"Jake! Jake!" Neil yelled.

"They're OK," Max said. "They're only playing."

But in his mind, Neil could see a yawning gap open up in the ice, and his beloved dog sliding helplessly into dark water. He couldn't help remembering the day Sam died, when Jake had been carried away in the river.

Jake would have drowned that day if it hadn't been for Sam. He'd given his own life as his damaged heart failed in the fight to pull Jake to safety. Part of

Neil knew he was being superstitious, but he could see the whole horrible accident happening again.

"Jake! Here!" he yelled.

Out on the ice, Jake stopped, ears cocked. Prince dashed up to him and playfully hurled himself on top of the young Border collie; the two dogs rolled over and over together.

"Jake! Come here!"

Neil knew that he ought to go and grab Jake, but when he thought about putting his weight onto the ice he felt sick. Even though he could see it was thick enough to support lots of other people, he still couldn't help imagining it splintering, plunging him into the lake.

He was taking a breath to shout again when Jake got to his feet, shook himself, and began trotting obediently to the bank. As soon as Neil could grip his collar without venturing onto the ice, he clipped on his leash. "Heel, Jake. Now!"

He realized that Max was staring at him. "Hey, Neil, it's not . . ."

Neil took no notice. Then he heard Emily say under her breath, "Don't bother him, Max. It's because of what happened to Jake when Sam died. He nearly drowned, and so did Neil."

It was no help to Neil to realize that Emily understood. He felt hot and uncomfortable, as if he'd been caught doing something he shouldn't.

It was worse still when Max asked, "Neil, are you afraid of water now? Because —"

"I don't want to talk about it, OK?" Neil snapped.

He pulled at Jake's leash, and started to run along the path to the castle. As he was going he heard Emily say, "I think you're right, Max. He'll have to get over it, but it might take a long time."

CHAPTER FOUR

"*What do you want from me?*" said King Arthur. "*Speak.*"

The king and his noble knights were seated around the Round Table in the Great Hall at Camelot. Zeno walked forward from the doorway, with his faithful dog at his heels, and bowed low to the king.

"My Lord Arthur," he said, "Queen Morgan le Fay has stolen something valuable from me. I need your help to get it back."

King Arthur gravely stroked his beard, while Sir Kay, his steward, leaned closer to him and said, "My lord, how do we know this boy isn't a spy from Morgan?"

As Sir Kay spoke, Prince bounded down the length of the hall, hopped up onto an empty seat, and put his *front paws on the Round Table to bark indignantly at him. The other knights laughed.*

"Prince is so cool!" Neil murmured.

Along with Emily and Penny, he was sitting in the minstrels' gallery above the hall, watching the scene that was being shot below. He never stopped being amazed at how perfectly trained Prince was, and how he always seemed to know what he was supposed to do.

"And look at Fred!" said Emily, pointing at the huge wolfhound sprawled lazily in front of the fireplace. "He's pretty good, too."

Down below, Sir Lancelot was rising to his feet, but instead of getting on with the scene, he looked around for Brian Mason, and said, "Brian, I don't think this scene is right."

"Cut!" Brian yelled at the camera crew. "What's the matter now, Brett?"

"Well, everybody knows that Sir Lancelot was Arthur's best knight," said Brett Benson. "I think I should have a line there, instead of the silly business with the dog."

Brian Mason banged down his clipboard. Some of the knights started to mutter among themselves. The actor playing Sir Kay put his chin on his hands and said, "Here we go again!"

"Brett," said Brian, "I thought up that 'silly business' with the dog, along with Maggie Brown and the scriptwriters. Can't you understand that, in this film, it's the dog who's the star?"

Brett Benson looked furious. "Then if the dog's the star, you obviously don't need an actor of my talents. Find yourself another Sir Lancelot!"

His chair scraped on the flagstones as he pushed it back and marched out of the hall. Brian Mason took a deep breath, called, "OK, folks, take five!" and hurried after him.

"Oh, no!" said Emily. "They've stopped filming again. They're never going to finish at this rate."

"I'm going down to talk to Max," said Neil.

With Emily and Penny following, he ran down the steps from the gallery and into the hall. Max was standing near the fireplace, talking to Suzie and Maggie Brown, but when he saw Neil and the others, he came to meet them, with Prince trotting beside him.

Neil could see that Max was seething with fury.

"That was a really good take, until he ruined it!" Max fumed.

"Take it easy," Neil said. "It'll be just as good next time."

Prince made a soft whining sound and pushed his nose into Max's hand. Max relaxed a bit and stroked his head.

"Why don't you get another Sir Lancelot if Brett Benson is such a pain?" Penny asked.

"I wish we could!" Max said. "But that would mean

repeating all the scenes we've already shot. It would cost way too much, and Brett Benson knows it."

"And I used to be a fan of his!" Emily said indignantly.

"What really gets me," Max went on, "is that he doesn't care about the *film* at all. He only cares about Brett Benson. Honestly, if he —"

A voice interrupted him, shouting loudly from the passage outside. "Max! Where's Max gone? Max!"

Neil turned around. In the hall doorway stood Jeff Calton. His hair was untidy and his face was red with anger. He had a stack of tattered papers in one hand, and in the other, held by the scruff of the neck, was Princess. A shred of white paper was dangling from the little pup's jaws.

Princess was whimpering. Max stormed over to Jeff Calton and took her away from him. "Don't hold her like that! You're hurting her!"

"Then look after her properly!" Jeff yelled back at him. "Look what's she done!"

He brandished the papers in Max's face. Max took a step back, holding Princess close to him. "These are my production notes. They're vital. Now I'll have to do all of them again because your puppy chewed them up."

Neil came to stand beside Max. Princess was trembling, and trying to hide her head in the crook of Max's arm.

"Hang on a minute," Neil said. "Everybody knows

that pups chew things. If you left your notes lying around, Mr. Calton, you're just as much to blame as Princess."

Jeff Calton stared at him as if he didn't remember who he was. "Those notes were left in a file in my bedroom," he snapped. "With the door closed."

"Then how did Princess get at them?" Max asked.

"How should I know? When I went up there just now, she was in the middle of the floor making a meal of them. You simply can't have her here, Max, if you can't take better care of her than that."

Max went red at the suggestion that he couldn't take care of his dog. His hand shaking, he stroked Princess and said nothing.

"It's not Max's fault," Emily said, coming to stick up for him. "He was on the set."

"Then who was supposed to be looking after the dog?"

"Adrian," said Penny. "He offered to look after Princess and Jake."

Neil began to think he understood. Adrian Bartlett was a whiz at taking charge of Lord Ainsworth's business affairs, but a little vague about everything else. Princess might well have wandered away from him, but that still didn't explain how she managed to get into Jeff Calton's bedroom, or open the file.

"So where is Adrian now?" Jeff asked.

Adrian Bartlett himself answered the question by walking through the doors as Jeff was speaking. He

wore his outdoor clothes, and had Jake on a leash.
He smiled at Neil as he handed the young dog over,
stamped his feet on the floor to warm them up, and
asked, "Is there a problem?"

Jeff launched into a long complaint about his ruined notes.

"I'm so sorry," Adrian said when he had finished.
"Jake needed a walk, and Princess was asleep in her
basket in the kitchen, so I left her there. We were
only gone twenty minutes or so."

"And you remembered to shut the door, I suppose?"
Jeff said sarcastically, not waiting for an answer.
"I've had just about enough of this," he went on. "I'm
going to phone Manchester and get a couple more security staff sent down. From now on, nothing's going
to happen around here unless I say so."

He spun around, but his dramatic exit was spoiled
when he nearly tripped over Jake, who barked in
protest as he darted to one side.

"Dogs!" Jeff Calton snarled. "I've had dogs up to
here!"

He strode out.

Adrian looked after him with a bewildered expression. "I did shut the door," he said. "I don't know how
she managed to get out."

"It's not your fault," Penny said loyally. "He must
have left the notes lying around, no matter what he
says."

But Neil wasn't so sure. He knew how efficient Jeff

Calton was. "Max, you know what you told us, about the accidents?"

"You've been pretty unlucky, haven't you?" Emily added.

"Well, yes . . ." said Max.

"It's just . . ." Neil began. He paused as he put two and two together and came up with an answer he didn't like at all. "Well, what if they're not accidents?"

"What do you mean?" asked Penny.

"I mean that they're happening too often. It just can't be a coincidence. It's almost as if somebody is doing it on purpose."

"They couldn't be." Max had turned pale.

"Oh, yes, they could," said Neil. "How do you think Princess managed to get into Jeff Calton's room, unless somebody put her there? How do you think she got the notes out of the file all by herself? Max . . ." He hesitated and then went on. "Max, can you think of anyone who would deliberately try to wreck this film?"

CHAPTER FIVE

Neil halted and stood panting, watching his breath puff out into the cold air. "Phew!" he gasped. "These branches are heavy!"

After the scene in the Great Hall was finally finished, he and Emily had gone into the woods with the dogs to cut greenery for Christmas decorations. Now they were pulling a sled back to the castle, loaded with holly and yew boughs and trailing strands of ivy.

Jake and Prince were frolicking about among the trees, and Princess sat in the middle of the branches, looking as proud as if she was riding in a royal coach. Neil was looking after the dogs for Max, so that Max could shut himself up in his bedroom and learn some lines for the following day.

Emily laughed, and picked up the sled rope that Neil had dropped. "Medieval peasants had to collect wood every day, you know."

"Well, I'm glad I'm not a medieval peasant then," Neil said, rubbing his aching back.

"But you're going to be," Emily said. "Max told me. Just as soon as they rebuild the village."

"Why am I always a peasant?" Neil complained. "Why don't I get to be a knight, or even a squire?"

"Or a huntsman with the hounds," Emily teased. Neil brightened up. "Yeah! That'd be cool!"

"Come on," said Emily. "Let's get back before we freeze. I'll pull for a while."

As they began slogging through the snow again, Emily asked, "Neil, are you really convinced that somebody's trying to spoil the filming?"

"Yes, I am."

"But who would do that?"

His sister didn't sound as if she expected an answer, but Neil gave her one. "I think it might be Brett Benson."

"Oh, him!" Emily sniffed. "I wouldn't be surprised. But if the film isn't made, he'll be out of a job."

Neil watched his feet crunching into the snow, as if that would help him concentrate. "I didn't want to say this in front of Max, but most of the things that have gone wrong involve the dogs — Prince mostly, and now Princess as well. And who around here can't stand Prince?"

"Brett Benson!" said Emily.

"Right. Maybe he thinks that if he causes enough trouble, Prince will be out of the film and he'll be the star."

"But that doesn't make sense! It's a *Time Travelers* film. Prince has to be in it."

"You know that. I know that. The whole world and his dog knows that," Neil said. "But does Brett Benson know it? He doesn't act like he does. I figure he keeps delaying the filming, just because —"

Neil broke off as he heard frantic barking from among the trees where the dogs had been playing. Princess started yapping in reply.

"That sounds like Prince!" Neil said. "I wonder what's wrong. Em, keep an eye on Princess."

He left the path and plunged into the snow under the trees. "Prince! Prince, here, boy!"

The cocker spaniel came dashing out from behind a bramble thicket, snow spraying from his paws as he hurtled along. When he saw Neil he stopped barking, ran to meet him, and stood panting and trembling by his side.

Neil reached down and ruffled his fur. "What's the matter, boy?"

Emily dropped the sled rope and came to look. "Maybe he's cut one of his paws, or picked up a thorn," she suggested.

"He wasn't limping," Neil replied. He ran a hand down Prince's flank. The spaniel was standing quietly now, and seemed to be settling down. Neil was mystified. "I'll take a look." He began to retrace Prince's tracks through the snow.

He had started to worry about where Jake was, but as he skirted the bramble thicket he heard the young collie barking playfully. When Jake came into sight, he was bounding around a figure in medieval costume who was holding a branch up for Jake to leap and snap at. Neil recognized the extra who had helped Prince when the village inn collapsed.

"Hi!" he called. "Did you see what —"

The extra turned, saw him, threw the branch down, and ran off through the trees. Jake gave a bark of protest that his game had ended so abruptly, then pounced on the branch and held it up for Neil. Neil squatted down to rub his head. "OK, boy?" he said. "Was that weird or what?"

The extra couldn't have done anything to hurt Prince, or Jake wouldn't have played so happily with him. But something had upset the cocker spaniel. Neil wished the man had stayed so he could have asked what it was.

He straightened up and went back to where Prince and the others were waiting for him. Jake trotted along beside him. "I wish you could talk, boy," Neil said. "Maybe you could make some sense out of what's going on around here."

By the following morning the repairs to the damaged building were finished, so filming could start again in the village. Jeff Calton sent Neil and Emily to the wardrobe person to be fitted out with peasant costumes.

"The wardrobe is in a room off the Long Gallery," Max explained as he led the way up the spiral staircase. Prince was with him, and he was carrying Princess tucked into the crook of his arm. The cocker spaniel pup was too small to keep up with them on the stairs, but Neil thought Max was secretly pleased to have an excuse to cuddle her.

Prince had completely recovered from whatever had spooked him in the woods, and was his usual cheerful self, bounding ahead of Max up the stairs. Neil had left Jake with Maggie Brown — he didn't feel confident that the excitable young dog would behave himself among all the costumes.

As they reached the top of the stairs, they almost bumped into Adrian Bartlett, who was hurrying along in the other direction.

"Adrian," said Max, "would you mind keeping an eye on Princess again? I've got to go down to the village set."

"What?" Adrian was looking flustered, as if he had something else on his mind. "Oh — Princess. Yes, of course, Max. Should I take her now?"

"Please." Max handed Princess over, and the little dog put her paws on Adrian's chest and licked his face enthusiastically, dislodging his glasses. "She likes you," said Max.

"Er . . . yes." Adrian gave Max a distracted smile and darted off down the stairs, carrying Princess.

"What's bugging him?" said Neil.

Nobody answered.

The Long Gallery was a wide corridor on the second floor of Ainsworth Castle. On one side, windows looked out over the lake. Rooms led off the other side, and through one open door Neil saw props and coats of armor for the film — helmets and swords and shields and a whole rack of chain-mail tunics.

Hanging on the gallery walls were huge paintings in heavy gold frames. Neil lagged behind to look at them. Most were portraits of men and women in old-fashioned dress, and featured dogs that looked just like King. Neil remembered that King's line of Great

Danes had been the special companions of the Ainsworth family for hundreds of years.

Just then he heard Emily calling to him from farther down the gallery. "Come on, Neil, we're waiting for you!"

Neil hurried along to join her at the door of a larger room at the far end. One wall was lined with costumes, and at the other side there was a sewing machine and ironing board, and screens for the cast to change behind. Max was just disappearing with his Zeno costume, and Prince sat quietly down to wait for him as people rushed in and out of the changing area.

Brett Benson was also there, wearing a blue velvet tunic with long scalloped sleeves, and smirking at himself in a mirror.

"This belt's wrong," he said. "Find me another, Verity."

The wardrobe person stopped sorting among the costumes on the rack. She was a slender young woman with short, dark curls. She had a friendly smile for Neil and Emily, but she sounded exasperated as she said, "OK, Brett. Just as soon as I've outfitted these peasants."

Brett swung around, looking bad-tempered. "Why do I have to wait for these kids?"

"Because they're due on the set," Verity said patiently. "You're not." She ignored Brett's snort of annoyance as she held up a mud-colored dress in front of Emily. "That looks about right. Sorry it's not very exciting. Now you," she went on, sizing up Neil with a practiced eye. "I believe I've got —"

"Verity," a voice from the doorway interrupted her, "is my costume ready?"

Verity ran her hands through her curls. The woman who had spoken was tall and striking, with long, dark hair and a pale, haughty-looking face.

"That's Morgan le Fay," Emily murmured to Neil. "The evil enchantress."

Neil nodded.

"You were going to take the seam in," Morgan reminded Verity. "Did you have time to do it? Jeff wants to shoot that scene today."

"Yes, I did it." Verity had begun to hunt along the rack, rattling the hangers along the rails as she searched. "That's funny. I'm sure I put it here."

Neil glanced at Emily, remembering how Max had told them that part of his costume had disappeared. Brett Benson said nastily, "Lost something *again*, Verity dear?"

Neil saw Verity turn pink and start sorting through the costumes even faster. Then she stooped over a pile of black material on the floor. "Here it is. It must have slipped off the hanger."

She stood up with the dress in her hands and shook it out. Morgan gasped. Emily exclaimed, "Oh, no!"

The dress was long and flowing, made of a lot of separate layers of filmy fabric. The top layer was sewn with hundreds of tiny sequins. Neil could imagine it would make a stunning costume for a witch queen, except that all down the front of it were splashes of silver paint.

Verity was staring at the dress. She looked as if she was going to start crying. "I don't believe it. I just don't believe it!" she gasped.

Morgan went up to the dress and dabbed cautiously at the paint marks. "It's not dry yet," she said. "It can't be long since it was done. Verity, is there anything in here that could have gotten spilled?"

"No," said Verity. "What would I be doing with paint? It looks like the stuff the props people are using for the armor."

Neil spotted some splashes of paint on the floor where the dress had been, and then got down on his hands and knees to look under the costume rack. Catching sight of something in the shadows by the wall, he burrowed underneath and came out with a paint can in one hand. It was nearly empty, and it had sticky silver dribbles on the outside.

"Is this it?"

Both women looked at it, and Verity said, "It must be. But how did it get under there?"

"Have you been in here all morning?" Neil asked.

Verity looked flustered, as if she was trying to remember. "I came up after breakfast, and then I went back to my bedroom to fetch some sewing things. . . . It could have happened then, I suppose."

"What could have happened?" It was Jeff Calton's voice; the producer was standing in the doorway. "Where are my peasants? We need to — Oh, good grief, just look at that!"

He had caught sight of the dress, which Verity was still holding up. Striding into the room, he examined the paint marks, and let out a long sigh, as if he could barely keep control of his temper. "OK, Verity," he said quietly, "see if it can be cleaned. I'll reschedule the scene. Neil, Emily, get changed and down to the village set right away. Max . . . Where's Max?"

"Here," said Max, emerging from behind the screens in his Zeno costume. As if he couldn't help himself, he added, "At least nobody can blame this on Prince or Princess."

"I wouldn't be too sure," Brett Benson said. He had been lounging against the wall beside the mirror, watching everything with a spiteful smile on his face. Now he came forward and bent over Prince.

Prince backed away, but Brett Benson grabbed him and rubbed some of the feathery hairs on Prince's legs between his finger and thumb. When he showed his hand to Jeff Calton, there were silver marks on it.

"If Prince had nothing to do with it," he said, "then why is there paint on him?"

CHAPTER SIX

Max pushed himself between Brett Benson and his dog. "Leave Prince alone!"

He squatted down and put an arm around Prince's neck. Neil stooped beside him and examined the cocker spaniel's coat. Brett Benson was right — there were flecks of silver paint around Prince's front paws.

Jeff Calton ran a hand through his hair. "Honestly, Max, it's just one thing after another. Can't you keep your dogs under control?"

"Obviously not," said Brett Benson. "But if you have kids and dogs hanging around on the set, what can you expect?"

He cast another glance at himself in the mirror, and strolled out into the gallery, still smirking.

"Prince *is* under control!" Max said hotly. "He didn't spill the paint. I know he didn't!"

"Then how did it get on him?" Jeff asked.

"I don't know!"

"Listen, Mr. Calton," Neil said. He was finding it easier than Max to keep calm. After all, it wasn't his dog in trouble. "Just think about it. Verity says the props people are using this paint. Do you think Prince went into the props room, found the paint, and carried it back here, just so he could spill it on a costume? And then hide the paint can under the rack? It's just not possible. It doesn't make sense."

"I don't know what makes sense anymore," Jeff said, exasperated. "I just know that this film will be ruined if there's any more trouble. Anyway, Max, and you two — village set in fifteen minutes, OK?"

He strode out. Morgan gave Verity a quick hug and said, "Don't worry," before following him. Emily went behind the screens to change, while Verity put the ruined dress to one side and went back to looking for Neil's costume.

"Max," Neil said while he waited, "where was Prince this morning? Has he got an alibi for this?"

Max frowned, thinking. "I'm not sure. I fed him in the kitchen first thing, and then I left him there while I went to breakfast. I suppose he could have wandered up here."

"But he didn't fetch the paint from the props room," Neil said. "Somebody else did. Then they spilled the paint on the dress and dabbed some on Prince so that he would get the blame."

Max was looking even more upset now. He was still kneeling beside Prince, an arm around him. "I'm not taking my eyes off Prince after this," he said. "Whoever it is, they'd better not try anything else!"

He straightened up. "Neil, I'm going down to makeup. I'll see you on the set. Come on, Prince." He slapped his leg, and Prince trotted obediently after him.

Neil watched him go, and then realized that Verity was holding out his costume: a pair of loose brown pants and a shirt, with a sheepskin tunic to go on top.

"Thanks," he said absentmindedly. As he went off to change, he was still thinking about the attempts to sabotage the film and whether there was anything he could do to put a stop to them.

The collapsed inn had been repaired, and the village looked very realistic under its coating of snow. Brian Mason wanted to film one of the most important scenes of the episode, in which the villagers, who had been forced to work for the wicked Morgan le Fay, rebelled, joining King Arthur and his knights in an attack on her castle.

"You can't have found *another* castle for Morgan?" Neil said to Max.

"No, it's just a different part of this one," Max explained. He still sounded tense, and he kept Prince very close beside him while they waited for filming to begin. "But it'll look fine on the film."

Nearby, King Arthur and his knights were mounting their horses, getting ready for the moment when they were to come trotting into the village. The villagers had to cheer them and then listen while Arthur rallied them to fight against the wicked Morgan.

The director called the extras together and explained how the scene would work. While he was talking, Neil noticed the mysterious extra standing in the back of the crowd, head down, as if he didn't want to be seen. Neil edged his way toward him.

"Hi," he said. "Thanks for getting Prince out the other day."

The man gave him a sideways glance and just grunted. Neil tried not to let the gruff manner put him off. This was the first real chance he'd had to talk to him, and he wanted to find out what had frightened Prince in the woods and why the man had run away.

"I saw you playing with my dog Jake in the woods," he said chattily. "Do you like dogs?"

Another grunt.

"Jake really enjoyed —" Neil was beginning, when a shout from Brian Mason interrupted him. "Shut up in the back there, will you? We haven't got all day!"

Neil had to give up and start paying attention to the scene.

King Arthur and his knights rode in, wearing bright surcoats and shining armor. Brett Benson as Sir Lancelot carried a scarlet-and-gold banner. Neil and Emily and all the other villagers cheered, and Zeno came forward to offer their support to Arthur.

The run-through went perfectly, and Brian decided to go for a take. The horsemen regrouped and rode into the village again, but when the time came for Max to talk to the king, Prince suddenly broke out into frantic barking, and tore off down the path toward the castle.

"Cut! Cut!" Brian yelled. "Somebody catch that dog!"

Max and Maggie Brown ran off together after Prince. Neil followed, fishing in his pocket under his costume for a dog treat to help coax the cocker spaniel back. By the time he caught up, Maggie already had a hand on Prince's collar, and Max was patting his dog to soothe him.

He looked up as Neil approached. "Something bothered him. He's not usually like this."

Neil squatted down and offered the tidbit to Prince, who wolfed it down and looked for more. He had recovered from his shock, whatever it was, and trotted happily back toward the set at Max's heel.

Neil wondered whether to say something to Max about the extra. He didn't think that anyone else had noticed, but the man had been right next to Prince just before the dog took off. Prince had behaved exactly as he had in the woods the day before when they had met the man. It looked as if Prince didn't like him, but Neil didn't understand why.

The next take went well, but Brian Mason insisted on filming the scene a second time anyway. When he was satisfied, Neil and Emily went back to the castle to wash off their makeup and change into regular clothes. Then they headed for the kitchen to find Jake. The young Border collie threw himself at Neil to welcome him, leaping up with his tongue lolling out in a doggy grin.

"Hey, get down, you goofy dog!" Neil rumpled Jake's ears. "I've been away two hours, not two months!"

The kitchen at Ainsworth Castle was a huge room, with oak beams holding up a whitewashed ceiling. Copper pans hung on the walls, decorated with sprigs of holly from the greenery Neil and the others had collected the day before.

Along one side was an old-fashioned kitchen range, where Adrian Bartlett was making himself a cup of coffee. Princess was balancing on his shoe and trying to climb up his leg.

Adrian looked a bit agitated. "Is Max back?" he asked.

"No, he stayed to do another scene," said Neil. "Is Princess a problem?"

"I have to finish off the estate Christmas cards,"

Adrian explained. "And I shudder to think what she could get up to in the office! I don't dare leave her, though, especially after what happened yesterday."

"I'll look after her," Emily said, scooping up Princess and cuddling the little pup close to her face. "Come on, gorgeous."

Adrian gave her a relieved smile. "Thanks, that's a big help." He took his coffee and went out, pausing in the doorway to say, "Penny's putting up decorations in the small drawing room, if you want to give her a hand."

The "small" drawing room was about the size of a tennis court. When Neil and Emily arrived, Penny was sorting shiny baubles in a large cardboard box. An enormous Christmas tree, without any decorations, stood in a tub on one side of the fireplace with a stepladder next to it. A bright fire was burning, and the room smelled of pine branches.

"Hello," Penny said, smiling. "I could use some help. Better keep the dogs away, though. If they break these, they could get hurt."

"Jake should be OK," Neil said, as the Border collie went to touch noses with King, who was sprawled on the rug in front of the hearth. "Em, you'd better hang on to Princess."

Emily gave him a blissful smile. "No problem!"

Neil went up the ladder and Penny handed him the baubles.

"How did the filming go?" she asked.

"OK," said Neil. "But it was freezing cold down there. You're lucky your scenes are indoors!"

Penny laughed. "I have to do embroidery, though!" Pausing with a glittering ball in one hand, she added, "Was there any trouble?"

Emily was sitting cross-legged on the rug, while Princess scrambled all over her and covered her face with sloppy licks. She said, "Not really. But we think that extra — the one Neil saw in the woods — might have spooked Prince a bit."

"I wonder who he is," said Neil. "Penny, do you know him?"

Penny shook her head. "Most of the extras are village people, but I've never seen him before."

Neil reached down for another bauble and fastened it carefully to a branch. "It's weird, because he helped Prince when the set collapsed, and he got along fine with Jake. I can't understand why Prince has taken a disliking to him."

Penny shrugged. "Oh, well . . . That's not the big problem, though. What I want to know is, who's trying to wreck the film? Verity told me what happened with the paint."

"Brett Benson was up there," Emily said. "And he was the one who found the paint spots on Prince."

Penny frowned and shook her head. "I can't believe it's him. Nobody's that stupid!" She fished in the box again. "Here's the star to go on top. Can you reach that far, Neil?"

Neil took the star and climbed up to stand precariously at the top of the ladder. While he leaned over to fix the star to the uppermost branch of the tree, he said, "I've been thinking. Whoever's doing this has to be able to come and go in the castle without anybody asking questions."

"That means the whole of the film crew," said Emily.

"And the people who live here," said Neil.

"But none of us would do it!" Penny protested. "We want the film to be made. The money's going to pay for all sorts of things."

Neil still wasn't used to the idea that a lord who owned a castle could be short of money, but he knew that Penny was right. Lord Ainsworth really needed the fee from the production company.

"Yes, but . . ." An idea was nagging at Neil. A few things he'd ignored were starting to fit together. "You know, Adrian was up in the Long Gallery at about the time the paint was spilled. He looked a bit funny, too, as if he didn't want to be seen up there."

"But Adrian's nice!" Emily protested. "And he was happy about the film from the start."

"I know." Neil tweaked the star into position and climbed down to where he felt safer. "But that's not the only thing. He was supposed to be looking after Princess yesterday when she got into trouble for chewing Jeff Calton's notes."

"He took Jake for a walk," said Emily.

"I just wonder if that's the only thing he did."

Penny had stopped unpacking the decorations and stood still, staring up at Neil. "That's . . . ridiculous," she said. "Why would Adrian try to spoil the film?"

"Not spoil it," said Neil. "Just delay it. You said yourself, your dad needs the money. And the longer the film crew are here, the more they'll have to pay for using the castle. I'm sorry, Penny. I'm really sorry. But Adrian —"

Penny had suddenly gone red with anger. "It's not Adrian — he wouldn't! I know he wouldn't! You are so arrogant, Neil Parker. You always think you're right, but really you don't know anything. I think you're horrible!"

She spun around and ran out of the door, slamming it behind her.

CHAPTER SEVEN

"Neil, you're so insensitive," said Emily. The sound of the banging door drifted away. "How could you say all that in front of Penny?"

Neil came down the ladder. He felt awful. "I was just thinking out loud," he said. "I didn't want to upset her, but it's true, all the same. It could be Adrian. He's Lord Ainsworth's steward — it's his *job* to keep an eye on everything. He can go anywhere he likes in the castle and nobody thinks twice about it. He might even think that it's not really wrong, because the money would help Lord Ainsworth." He paused, and when Emily didn't say anything he challenged her. "Don't you think I'm right?"

Emily was still playing with Princess, running the

little dog's silky ears through her fingers. "Maybe," she replied. "But it's hard to believe."

"I like Adrian as well," Neil said defensively. "But if he's innocent, why did he look so guilty this morning?"

Emily didn't answer. Neil put the lid back on the box of decorations. They couldn't carry on without Penny, and with so much bad stuff happening it was difficult to feel the usual excitement of Christmas. He remembered that in another two days they were supposed to be going home. He wasn't even sure that he would enjoy his own Christmas at King Street if he had to leave an unsolved mystery behind him. The argument with Penny made it even harder. Neil couldn't help thinking it was going to be the most miserable Christmas of his life.

The buffet lunch for the film crew was soup and sandwiches in the castle dining hall. Actors and crew were sitting on either side of the long dining table. Neil hoped to see Penny, because he wanted to apologize, but there was no sign of her. Making up would have to wait.

Max was there, drinking a mug of soup, with Prince sitting at his feet and looking up hopefully at the sandwich in his other hand. He grinned when he saw Neil and Emily.

"Hi. Things went really smoothly this morning. No problems at all."

"That's great." Neil fetched a plate of sandwiches to share with Emily, and they found themselves seats.

"I see you've got Princess," Max went on. "Thanks. Would you mind keeping her this afternoon? We're filming that scene again — the one where the inn collapsed."

"They better make sure it doesn't collapse again," Neil said, watching Emily give Princess a delighted hug.

"Jeff said he'd inspect it personally." Max drained his mug and put it down as Suzie, his chaperone, walked over, pointedly looking at her watch. "I'd better go. I'm due on set, and I have to visit makeup first."

He rushed off, followed by Prince. Neil fished a dog treat out of his pocket so that Jake wouldn't mind missing out on the sandwiches, and gave one to Emily for Princess.

"She's lovely!" said Emily. "Max is so lucky — apart from having to leave her and go off to film all the time. Oh, and wear all that yucky makeup!" She stroked the pup's tiny head. "We'll have fun, though, won't we, girl?"

"Makeup!" said Neil. He'd just thought of something, and he couldn't believe it hadn't occurred to him before. "You're right, it's disgusting stuff. Nobody goes around in their makeup unless they're in a scene."

"So?" said Emily.

"So what was that guy — that weird extra — doing in makeup yesterday? They were repairing the village set and none of the peasants were needed. But he was in the makeup room first thing in the morning, and later on, when we saw him in the woods, he was *still* in costume."

Emily was tickling Princess's stomach. The little dog lay on her lap with her paws in the air, wriggling happily. "Maybe he likes being a peasant."

"Get real, Em! This could be important. Whoever's doing this doesn't want to be noticed. If you see somebody wandering around in costume, you just assume he has to do with the film."

Emily started to take him seriously. "You mean he doesn't?"

"I don't know. But a peasant costume is a good disguise, with all that heavy makeup. Maybe he's wearing it so that nobody will recognize him."

"But why?" Emily asked. "What does he get out of wrecking the film?"

"We won't know that until we know who he is."

Neil felt like kicking himself. He'd wasted time suspecting Brett Benson, and he'd even upset Penny by accusing Adrian, when all the time the most likely solution was staring him in the face.

"Prince doesn't like him, either," Emily said. "He runs away from him!"

Neil nodded. "He knows something's wrong, Em. I really wish he could talk!"

"Prince the dog detective!" Emily said, laughing. "Hey, Princess . . . don't chew apart my sweatshirt!" The tiny pup had seized her sleeve cuff and was tugging at it, growling fiercely. Emily gently took it away from her. Suddenly looking serious, she went on, "OK, Neil, suppose you're right. What are we going to do?"

Neil's first instinct was to tell Brian Mason or Jeff Calton. But he'd gotten into enough trouble with Penny by not knowing when to keep quiet. This time he would have to be more careful.

"Whenever I've tried to talk to that extra, he's avoided me," he said. "This time I'm going to track him down. I'm going to find out who he is and what he thinks he's up to." He wolfed down the last of his sandwich and stood up. "Are you coming?"

"Just try to stop me!" Emily replied, gathering up Princess in her arms. Jake followed them.

On the way to grab their coats, they passed the old scullery that was being used as a makeup room. The door was open, and the same makeup girl was there, tidying away sticks of greasepaint.

Neil raised his eyebrows at Emily, who gave him a nod. "Hi," he said, going in. "Do you remember, yesterday — really early — you were making up one of the peasants? I wondered whether —"

"Now look," the girl interrupted. "I've told you before, I've got a job to do here. I don't want you in this room unless you're being made up. And I certainly haven't got time to answer stupid questions."

She turned away. Neil could still see her face in the mirror. It looked hot and angry.

He said, "Sor-*ree,*" and left the room. "You see?" he said to Emily. "There *is* something weird about that guy — and I bet she knows what it is!"

Muffled in coats and scarves, Neil and Emily trudged across the stone bridge and down the footpath toward the village set. Snow had started to fall again. Princess, tucked up in her favorite place inside Emily's jacket, licked at snowflakes that fell on her nose.

"This is what I think," said Neil. Jake followed him at ankle level. "We've got Princess, so he can't try anything with her, which means he's going to be hanging around where Prince is."

Instead of going straight down the path to the set, Neil steered them into the woods, working his way around toward the trailers on the far side. He thought they would have to hang around for a while, but as they emerged from behind the location catering van on the edge of the set, they almost collided with the extra going the other way.

Jake gave a welcoming bark and bounced up to

him. The extra ignored him, but Neil got his first really good look at the man's face. He couldn't help feeling that he should recognize him.

"Hello," he said. "I didn't know the peasants were filming today."

The extra turned away, muttering something.

"Just a minute," Neil said, wanting to delay him as he tried to remember where he had seen him before. The man ignored him, and started to walk away.

Emily said determinedly, "We wanted to ask you something. Are you —"

"Get lost. I'm busy," the man interrupted, an irritable expression on his face.

The bad-tempered look suddenly reminded Neil. He stood there gaping. When he spoke, he wasn't sure that his voice was going to come out right. "Harry Jenkins! That's who you are!"

The man ducked his head, and gave him a shifty look. "Don't know what you're talking about."

"Oh, yes, you do," Neil said. "I remember you now. You're Harry Jenkins. You were Prince's dog trainer when they filmed *The Time Travelers* at Padsham Castle."

Emily's eyes were like saucers. "Neil, you're right! I don't believe it!"

Neil went on. "Yes, you nearly wrecked that episode because you couldn't handle Prince. Are you trying to wreck this one as well?"

Harry Jenkins didn't answer.

Neil was furious. Prince had taken the blame last time as well, until the truth had come out. "Does Jeff Calton know that you're on the set?" he asked. "I bet he doesn't. But he will soon."

"We'll see to that!" Emily added.

"Interfering kids," Harry Jenkins said. "It was your fault I had to leave my job last time." He prodded Neil in the chest. "I haven't worked since. Everybody knows what happened, and nobody will give me a job as a dog trainer now. So I signed on as an extra. So what?"

Neil almost felt sorry for him. Last time he'd lost his nerve because a dog had bitten him, and that wasn't his fault. But he had been wrong to try to carry on with his job and then blame his problems on Prince. And Neil was beginning to feel certain that Harry Jenkins was to blame for all the recent disasters.

"That's not all, is it?" he asked. "You're not just an extra. Is it you who's been causing all the trouble? Just so you can get back at Prince for what happened? Did you mess with the stairs on the set, so the whole thing would fall apart? Did you put Princess where she could chew Mr. Mason's notes, and —"

"I don't know what you're talking about," Harry Jenkins interrupted.

"I think you do."

"No wonder Prince doesn't like you," Emily said. "He knew who you were all along!"

"It's got nothing to do with me," Jenkins insisted. "I just needed the job. And if you go around saying it's my fault, you'll find yourselves in trouble. So keep your mouths shut!"

He shoved Neil to one side and stormed off through the trees.

The man's stern words didn't frighten Neil. He stood watching Jenkins until he was out of sight, and then whistled for Jake, who had run a few paces after him and now stood looking back as if he didn't understand what was going on.

"We've got to tell somebody," said Emily, gently soothing Princess, who was still tucked down her front.

"Right," said Neil. "Brian Mason's on the set, so let's go and look for Jeff Calton. We've got to make him see that none of these accidents are the dogs' fault."

When they got back to Ainsworth Castle, Jeff Calton was standing at the end of the stone bridge, talking to a couple of people in a car. They were in uniform; Neil thought they must be the security staff Jeff had sent for.

He gave Emily a glance and went up to speak to him. "Mr. Calton —"

Jeff Calton didn't look at him. "Not now, Neil."

"But this is important."

"I said not now. I have to brief these people."

"But —"

Ignoring him, Jeff got into the car and said to the driver, "Straight ahead. I'll show you where to park."

The car took off, across the stone bridge and under the arch into the castle courtyard.

"Well!" said Emily indignantly.

Neil stared after the car in frustration. He'd solved the mystery of why so much was going wrong with the film, and now the producer wouldn't listen to him. How long would it be before Harry Jenkins thought of something else to do?

Then he heard a voice calling his name. He turned to see Max and Prince making their way up from the village. "It went great!" Max said, smiling. "Brian was really pleased." He tickled Princess on her nose. "Hi there, midget! Have you missed your dad?" Then his smile vanished as he saw the expression on Neil's face. "Is something the matter?"

"You bet. Listen to this."

As they walked toward the castle and Neil talked, he could see that Max was getting just as furious as he was feeling himself. "Harry Jenkins!" he said. "He nearly got Prince dropped from the show! And this time it's worse — Prince could have been hurt."

He squatted down in the courtyard and hugged Prince. Prince, not understanding, put his paws up on Max's knee and slurped his tongue across his face.

Max laughed. "Oh, Prince, you're great!" Then he looked up at Neil, his laughter vanishing. "What do you think we should do?"

"We've got to make somebody listen," Emily said indignantly. "We've got to get rid of that man somehow."

"Where's Brian Mason?" Neil asked.

"Still on set. He's filming a scene with Morgan and the Black Knight."

"Then we'll tell him when he's finished. He'll have to do something. And while we're waiting . . ." he paused, "let's give the dogs a good run!"

Neil hung around in the castle courtyard while Max changed out of his costume. Emily had gone to find Penny, to tell her everything and make up. Neil was sorry he had ever suspected Adrian, and he hoped that Adrian himself would never find out. All the same, he still wanted to know why the steward had been so flustered that morning in the Long Gallery.

Jake gave a welcoming bark as Max and Prince hurried down the steps from the main castle entrance. Max was carrying Princess, but he put her down once he was in the courtyard. She sniffed at the slush and tried to shake it off her paws, then skidded after Jake and Prince as they headed out under the archway.

"That's better," said Neil. "They haven't had a good run all day."

He was beginning to get over his anger as he followed the dogs across the stone bridge and took the footpath that ran alongside the lake. It was good to get out with Jake and forget about the problems of the filming.

Max felt the same, Neil was sure. After a few minutes he found a stick for the dogs to chase. Both Prince and Jake bounded after it, barking madly and sending up flurries of snow. Princess scampered along after them, adding her high-pitched yapping, her floppy ears flying up and down.

Max laughed as Prince brought the stick back to him, feathery tail wagging. "Good boy! Let Jake have a go this time. Go, Jake — fetch!"

"Oh, no!" Neil exclaimed. "Look at Princess!"

The little pup had given up the race for the stick. Someone had built a snowman by the lake, and

Princess hurled herself at it with shrill barks of delight, tugging at the brightly colored scarf around its neck. As she pulled, the head of the snowman rolled off and plumped down into the snow, half-burying the tiny dog.

"Hey, she'll hurt herself!" Max said, running toward her.

"No, she's fine!" Neil ached from laughing as he watched Princess scrabble out of the snowdrift with the scarf draped around her neck.

Max scooped her up and took the scarf off. "Naughty! Look what you've done."

He put her down and she scurried off again, dancing around in circles as if she was trying to catch her own tail, before dashing off to join her dad and Jake, who were hunting around the roots of some bushes near the lakeshore.

The lake was still covered with ice, and on the surface there were marks where people had been sliding and skating.

Neil was just going to suggest to Max that they should be getting back when the three dogs broke away from the bushes and ran out onto the ice. Prince was in the lead, with Jake close behind and Princess scampering along at the rear.

"Jake! Hey, Jake!" Neil yelled. Once again he could see in his mind the ice cracking to swallow up his dog in the dark water. "Jake, come here!"

Jake didn't come. Max shouted for Prince. The

cocker spaniel stopped and then came trotting back, but Jake and Princess stayed out on the ice, jumping around each other and gradually moving farther and farther away from the shore.

As Prince came panting up, Max took out his leash and clipped it on. Neil was psyching himself up to go out there and fetch Jake when Max thrust the loop of Prince's leash into his hand.

"I'll get them," he said.

Neil managed a weak smile. "Thanks."

He stood watching with Prince beside him as Max walked out onto the ice. Max kept calling the dogs, and eventually they both ran toward him. Neil saw him bend over to pick up Princess. Then, as he straightened up again, he seemed to stagger, and yelled something Neil couldn't catch. Jake started to bark. As Neil stared, transfixed, he saw a dark line open up in the ice, and Max went plunging down into the waters of the lake.

CHAPTER EIGHT

For a few seconds, Neil was panic-stricken. All his instincts told him to dash back to the castle, yelling for help. But then he came to his senses — help from the castle might be too late for Max and the dogs. Neil knew he had to do something now.

He stooped and unclipped Prince's leash. "Prince, go! Tell them at the castle!"

Prince looked up at him, whining softly, his intelligent eyes puzzled. Neil felt frustrated, not knowing exactly what commands Max used for Prince.

"Find Maggie," he said. "Go and fetch help! Go, Prince, go!"

He turned Prince's head toward the castle and gave the dog a gentle slap on the rump. Somehow

Prince must have understood, because he took off down the path, barking furiously as he ran.

Neil turned back to the lake. In spite of the gathering twilight, he could still see Max's head and shoulders, and a smaller black shape that he thought must be Jake. There was no sign of Princess at all.

His throat was dry. He told himself that he would only make things worse if he went out there to help. But he knew he couldn't just stand there and watch Max and the dogs drown because he was too scared to do anything.

A faint cry came across the ice from Max. "Help! Neil, get help!"

Desperately, Neil tugged a dead branch free from the undergrowth. Then, swallowing his fear, he crawled out onto the frozen lake on hands and knees so as not to put too much pressure on the fragile ice, pushing the branch in front of him.

He could see dark water slopping under the skin of ice. A few yards out from the shore he thought he could hear the ice start to creak, and, feeling it shifting under him, he lay flat and edged forward slowly on his stomach.

As he drew closer, he could see Max trying to grab the edge of the ice with one hand, but it kept breaking away. With his other hand he was clutching Princess. The little dog was limp, not moving.

Max was treading water, trying to keep afloat, but

Neil could see that he was already exhausted. His hair was soaking wet, as if his head had gone under at least once.

Close beside Max, Jake was standing on a piece of ice that had broken away from the rest. It floated, but water was washing over it. Jake's paws were splayed out as he fought for balance, and he was whining miserably.

"Max!" Neil yelled. "Here!"

Max saw him there for the first time. "Neil!" he gasped. "Keep back — it's all breaking up."

"Grab this." Neil pushed the branch out as far as he could so that Max could hang on to it and pull himself up to the edge of the ice. "Give me Princess!"

With something to grasp, Max managed to drag himself a little way out of the water and pass the pup across to Neil.

Princess looked unbelievably tiny with her coat plastered to her body. Her head lolled as Neil took her, and she didn't move.

"She's dead!" Max sobbed. "I know she's dead!"

"No, she's not," said Neil, though he couldn't tell.

Sprawled out on the ice, he couldn't do anything to help Princess or to get her warm. He yelled to Jake, but the collie couldn't get across to the main sheet of ice, and Neil couldn't reach him. He made one effort to grab Max's shoulders and haul him out, but when he tried, more of the surface near him cracked and water surged over it, soaking him through. The ice felt increasingly unsteady under him. He knew he couldn't go back now. All he could do was hang on.

"Prince went for help," he said to Max. "It won't be long."

He tried not to show how scared he was, for himself and Max, and especially for the dogs. Princess needed help quickly. Even if she was still alive, she wouldn't survive the cold for much longer.

Then, to his relief, Neil heard movement and voices from the lakeside. Someone shouted, "Don't move, Neil. We're coming!" and Neil tried to look over his shoulder, but his movement made the ice tilt alarmingly.

From then on, he kept as still as he could for what seemed like forever. Then he heard a voice much closer behind him. "Neil, move backward. There's a ladder here."

It was Adrian Bartlett. Neil felt almost too scared to move, but he edged back and felt hands guiding him until his feet made contact with the top rung of a ladder. He moved backward until he was lying on

it. Now he risked another glance over his shoulder
and saw that a system of ladders and planks had
been laid out for support across the ice.

Adrian moved forward on another ladder. He
gripped Max under the arms, helping him through
the splintering ice to the end of the ladder.

"Adrian!" Neil called. "What about Jake?"

"I'll get Jake." Adrian didn't turn to look at him.
"Go back to shore."

There was nothing Neil could do except obey.
Clutching Princess to him, he managed to crawl
backward until he reached the firmer ice at the edge
of the lake. Lord Ainsworth, Maggie Brown, and
Emily were waiting to help him back onto the shore.

"Maggie!" he gasped, shaking from cold as he held
out the little pup's limp body. "Look . . . we've got to
do something."

Maggie took Princess in firm, capable hands.

"Is she dead?" Emily asked, agonized.

Maggie pinched Princess's toes, and to Neil's delight he saw her eyelids twitch. A grin spread over
Maggie's face. "No, she's not dead."

Quickly, Maggie checked Princess's heartbeat,
then held her upside down by her back legs. Neil almost protested when he saw her dangling like that,
until he realized that water was trickling out of her
mouth.

Then Maggie laid Princess on her side, and opened
her mouth to pull her tongue forward and make sure

nothing was blocking her airway. "Got to get her breathing," she muttered.

Holding Princess's muzzle to keep her mouth closed, Maggie placed her own mouth around Princess's nose, and blew. Princess's chest rose and fell. Maggie took a breath and said, "Neil, check her heartbeat."

Neil laid his hand against Princess's side and nodded as he felt the faint fluttering. Maggie blew into her nostrils again. Again. And again.

"Princess!" Max appeared and collapsed to his knees beside the pup. He was soaked through and shivering convulsively, but he never took his eyes off her.

Neil kept his hand in place to monitor the heartbeat, and gave a cry of relief as he felt it strengthen. The rise and fall of Princess's chest became automatic as the little pup started breathing again.

He realized for the first time that Emily was crouched beside him, clutching painfully at his arm. She had tears on her face. "Will she be all right?" she asked Maggie.

"She'll be fine," Maggie promised. "But she needs warming up right now. I'll take her."

Carrying Princess, she set off to the castle at a run. Neil turned back to the lake. Relief flooded over him as he saw Adrian pulling Jake back onto dry land. When the steward carried him over, Neil thanked him and then squatted down beside the Border collie to put his arms around him.

"Jake, you dodo!" he said, but his voice was shaking and he had to make an effort not to cry. He couldn't face the thought of losing Jake as well as Sam. "Don't you dare do that again!"

When he was sure that Jake had come to no real harm, Neil also headed for the castle, the Border collie running alongside him. He and Max caught up with Maggie in the small drawing room. She was gently toweling off Princess in front of the fire. Princess's eyes were still closed, but she was breathing normally and her coat was already dry.

King and Fred were both sitting beside the fire, looking down at Princess almost as if they were guarding her.

Neil took one of the towels and rubbed Jake dry. The young Border collie seemed quieter than usual, but Neil didn't think there was much wrong with him. He'd been lucky to have escaped the worst of the freezing water.

Max stooped over Princess and stroked her. "Thanks, Maggie," he said unsteadily. "And you, Neil. I really thought she was dead."

"The vet's on his way," said Maggie. "But you're really not helping, standing there dripping over her. Go and get into some dry clothes."

Max struggled to smile, but he was still shivering and his teeth were chattering with cold. Neil grabbed him and propelled him out of the room. "Come on. Or they'll be holding up the filming for *you* this time."

When Neil and Max had changed, they went back to the drawing room, where Penny was serving hot drinks to the rescuers. Neil wrapped his hands around a mug of hot chocolate and took a gulp; the piping hot liquid brought tears to his eyes.

"Thanks," he said. "Er . . . Penny, I'm really sorry about what I said before. I know now it wasn't Adrian."

Penny gave him a hard look, and then she smiled. "I know — Emily told me. It's OK, Neil. It did look a bit suspicious." She glanced across the room to where Adrian was slumped in an armchair near the fire. "Now, go and thank him for pulling you out of the lake."

A wave of embarrassment flooded over Neil, almost as if Adrian knew what suspicions he'd had. "Yes, I will . . ." he said.

He was relieved to be able to put it off for a while, because he'd noticed the local vet, David Blackburn, bending over Princess by the fire. He was a blond-haired young man with big, gentle hands. Max was with him, and Neil went over to hear what the vet was saying.

"She'll sleep for a while now, and the best thing you can do is let her. Keep her quiet for a day or two. And if there are any problems, phone me right away. I'll be at home over the Christmas break."

He ran a hand over Princess's coat. The little spaniel stirred, opened her soft brown eyes to look at Max, and settled down again.

"She will be OK, won't she?" Max asked anxiously.

David smiled. "She'll be fine."

While the vet was busy giving Jake a checkup, Max's chaperone Suzie came in. "Max, the doctor's here to check you over."

Max looked up from Princess. "I'm OK, really."

"You're OK when the doctor says you are. You too, Neil. Or what will I tell your mom and dad?"

Neil and Max looked at each other and shrugged.

"All right." Max got up and went to the door, and

then stopped. "Just a minute," he said. "Where's Prince?"

Neil gazed around him as if he expected Prince to pop out from behind the nearest piece of furniture. In all the confusion, and the worry about Princess, he hadn't realized that the cocker spaniel wasn't around.

"I sent him up here for help," he said. "Somebody must have seen him."

"I was in the estate office when I heard him barking," Adrian said.

"But where did Prince go after that?" Max asked.

Maggie Brown remembered following Prince down to the lake with the other rescuers. Nobody had seen him since.

"He wasn't at the lake when I arrived," Adrian said. "I kept an eye out for him because I was afraid he would go out on the ice."

"He must be around here somewhere," Lord Ainsworth said. "We'd better look."

Efficiently, he divided everybody up into search teams to cover all of the castle. Suzie hauled Max off to the doctor, but Neil managed to slip away to join Penny and Emily, who were assigned to the Long Gallery and the rooms just off it. Though they carefully searched everywhere, they found no clues, and Prince did not answer when they called.

Suddenly, Neil noticed that there was a folded

sheet of paper lying on the Round Table in the Great Hall.

"What's that?" he asked.

Emily shrugged. "More production notes?"

Neil went over and picked up the paper, unfolded it, and stood staring. "Come and look at this!"

The others crowded around. The paper carried a message, written in black capital letters. It read:

I WANT £5,000. PUT IT IN THE HOLLOW TREE AT THE TOP OF THE LANE BY TOMORROW NIGHT. DON'T TELL THE PO-LICE, OR YOU WON'T SEE PRINCE AGAIN.

CHAPTER NINE

All the other searchers had already returned to the drawing room when Neil and the others went back with the ransom note. Max was there, too, with Princess sleeping on his lap, bundled up in a blanket; the tiny pup was twitching in her sleep. Max stroked her head. His mouth was tight, as if he was trying to hold in his worry.

"Look at this," said Neil. As they read the note, passing it from hand to hand, Neil explained what he suspected about Harry Jenkins.

"Jenkins!" Jeff Calton exclaimed. "I had no idea . . . I never even noticed that he was on set."

"That's because he was always in costume and makeup," Neil said. "He didn't want to risk being recognized. He must be out to wreck the film because he thinks it was Prince's fault that he lost his job as a dog trainer."

"That's garbage," Jeff said. "He lost his job because he couldn't cope and then tried to lie about it."

"So what do we do now?" Maggie asked.

Max had turned white. "I'll have to pay it. Or he'll kill Prince."

"But have you got five thousand pounds?" Penny asked. "It's an awful lot of money."

"I'm not sure . . . I think so. At least — what I earn from *The Time Travelers* goes into a fund for me, for later. There must be a way to get at it. I'm going to phone Dad."

He got up, gently set Princess down on the rug in front of the fire beside King and Fred, and went out.

Neil read the note again, as if it could tell him something else. As well as being anxious about Prince, he was starting to feel guilty. If he hadn't confronted Harry Jenkins, maybe he would have just gone on trying to find ways to disrupt the filming. That had been bad enough, but nothing like the disaster they were faced with now. Neil was afraid that he'd pushed Jenkins into one last effort to get revenge on the dog he thought had ruined his career.

And unless they could come up with an idea quickly, he was going to get away with it.

"We've got to get Prince back," Jeff Calton said, rubbing his hands through his hair until it stuck up in a crest. "We can't carry on filming until we do. I'll have a word with our security people."

"I'd call the police," said Lord Ainsworth. "They'll soon find —"

"No." The interruption came from Max, who had reappeared in the doorway. He looked tense and his voice was shaking. "If you do, he'll kill Prince. He says so."

He came into the room, sat on the rug beside Princess, and started to stroke the sleeping pup's silky head. "I talked to Mom," he said. "She and Dad will come down tomorrow, and see what they can do about the money."

Emily went to sit beside him. "We'll get Prince back," she said. "He'll be OK."

"Sure he will," said Jeff.

"Listen, Max," said Neil. "I don't think Harry Jenkins wants to hurt Prince. Remember, he helped to get him out when the village inn collapsed. He must have loved dogs once, or he wouldn't have been a trainer."

"He even played with Jake in the woods," Emily added.

Max said nothing, still intent on stroking Princess. Neil felt helpless. He didn't know what else they could do.

Beside the fire stood the Christmas tree. Somebody had finished decorating it, and the glass ornaments and tinsel glittered in the firelight. Neil could hardly believe it would be Christmas in a couple of days. He had too much on his mind to even think about it.

The silence was broken by Jeff Calton. "I'd better tell Brian. He's not going to like this."

"He can't call the police," Max said sharply.

"No, don't worry," Adrian said. "Nobody will do anything without talking to you first. Anyway, we could do without this kind of publicity."

When Jeff had gone, Neil flung himself into a chair and scratched Jake's ears as his dog padded up beside him. "I hate letting Harry Jenkins get away with it," he said. "It really bugs me, just thinking that he's got Prince somewhere —" He broke off. "Hey, that's it! Where *is* he keeping Prince?"

"Is he staying in the castle?" Emily asked.

Penny stared at her. "No, the extras aren't —" She stopped suddenly, as if she had just understood.

Adrian started to pace the room. "The principal actors and the film crew are all staying in the West Wing. We took on some more staff to look after them. The extras are local people, so they live at home and come in for the filming."

"Jenkins isn't a local," Maggie said. "So where is he staying?"

Neil sat up in his seat. "He must be somewhere close, so he can pick up the ransom. And it must be somewhere he could hide Prince . . ."

Max glanced up from stroking Princess, suddenly starting to look hopeful. "You really think we could find him?"

"What about a hotel?" Maggie asked.

"There's only the Ainsworth Arms in Beckthwaite," said Adrian.

Lord Ainsworth shook his head. "He wouldn't risk being seen with Prince."

"So where is he?" Penny asked.

"Wait a minute," said Neil. "What about that weird makeup girl? She knows something about Jenkins — I bet she does!"

"What makeup girl?" asked Maggie.

"We don't know her name," Emily explained. "But she was doing Jenkins's makeup when he wasn't supposed to be on set, and when we asked her about him she was really nasty!"

"Is she staying here?" asked Penny.

"She should be," said Adrian.

"There's one of the makeup assistants, called Shirley, in the room next to mine," said Maggie. "She's been very snappy ever since we arrived."

Neil sprang to his feet. "What are we waiting for?"

But when Maggie took them to Shirley's room, Shirley wasn't there, and when they asked some of the other makeup girls, no one knew where she was. Their only link to Harry Jenkins had disappeared.

*　　*　　*

"We're going home tomorrow," Emily said gloomily, winding her scarf around her neck.

"No, we're not," said Neil as he clipped Jake's leash onto his collar. "I'm not going anywhere until Max has Prince back."

As Neil got ready to walk Jake the following morning, he felt depressed. His brilliant idea had fizzled out. This morning, Shirley hadn't shown up for work. That was enough to make Neil certain she was involved with Harry Jenkins, but it didn't help in tracking either of them down.

The trail to Prince had gone cold, and without him, filming had come to a complete stop.

"But tomorrow's Christmas Eve," Emily pointed out. "We can't stay here for Christmas unless we're invited. Besides, Mom and Dad will freak out!"

"I don't care," Neil said determinedly. "I'm not leaving Max. Anyway, could you actually enjoy Christmas knowing Prince isn't safe?"

Emily shook her head. "I don't think anybody's going to enjoy Christmas!"

Neil pushed open the heavy oak door and looked out. Thick icicles hung from the top of the doorway; the steps and the courtyard were covered by a fresh fall of snow. At his feet, Jake whined uneasily, and tugged against the leash.

"Oh, no," Neil said. Even though he thought he'd overcome his own fear of water, he wasn't going to risk Jake on the ice again. "You're not running free today, boy. You're not going anywhere near that lake!"

He and Emily were venturing out into the snow when Max came along the passage with Princess on a leash. Neil was glad to see that the little pup was trotting along beside him, looking as perky as if the day before had been a dream.

"Hello there!" Emily said, crouching down to fondle the dog's long ears. "How is she, Max?"

"She seems fine. She's been whimpering a little, though. I think she misses Prince, and can't understand why he's not here."

Emily ruffled the pup's golden fur. "We'll find your dad, Princess, I promise!"

"What about the filming?" Neil asked.

Max shrugged. "Brian's talking about getting a stand-in for Prince, so we can carry on. But it won't be the same. I don't want to work with another dog."

Neil clapped him on the shoulder. "It's tough."

Max shrugged again. "Are you going out?" he asked. "I'll come with you. Maggie said it would be OK to take Princess out for a bit."

Before he had finished pulling on his thick jacket and boots, they were joined by Penny, who had both King and Fred beside her.

"I feel like harnessing these two to the sled," she said, laughing.

Neil couldn't help grinning, even though he was

worried. "With a sack and a Santa Claus outfit! That'd really be worth seeing!"

Penny put both the huge dogs on their leashes, and handed Fred's to Emily. They were heading out toward the lakeshore when Princess suddenly tugged on her leash and started whining.

"Maybe she's scared to go back down there," Emily suggested.

"It's OK," Max said, stooping to pick up the little dog. Princess evaded his hands, and started snuffling at something by the side of the path.

"Hang on a minute," Neil said. "Let's see what she does."

The spaniel pup kept her nose down for a minute, and then pulled on the leash in the direction of the medieval village. Neil and Max looked at each other.

"Do you think she knows something?" Max asked, as if he could hardly dare to believe it.

"She can't be tracking Prince," said Emily. "She's too little."

"Cocker spaniels have really good scenting skills," Neil said. "I think we should follow her."

They started to move down the path to the village, with Princess scuttling along in the lead, tail waving wildly. Then, as they approached the set, she hesitated, trotted back to Max, and away again to sniff at Jake.

"She's lost it," Max said, disappointed.

"Maybe, but I haven't," said Neil. "I've just remembered something . . . I think I know where Harry Jenkins is!"

"Where?" Max's voice was sharp with anxiety. "What do you mean?"

"The trailers by the medieval village." Neil pointed down the path to where the trailers were just in sight. "Look, Princess has practically brought us there. One of them is being used for makeup on the set. I bet Shirley's letting Harry stay in it!"

"We saw him in the woods that day," Emily added. "He could have been on his way there."

"And he was lurking around there when we met him yesterday," said Neil. "It's worth a try. Come on!"

CHAPTER TEN

They set off at a run toward the medieval village, the dogs bounding alongside. No one was on the set this morning, and the trailers looked quiet and deserted. As they paused on the edge of the village, Princess started barking, and danced around on the end of her leash.

"She knows her dad's here!" said Emily.

"Now what do we do?" asked Penny.

"I'm going to see who's in there," Neil said.

"No, wait . . ." Max sounded panicky, but Neil was already marching out into the clearing and across to the makeup trailer.

He rapped on the door. There was a moment's silence, then a scuffling noise from inside, and the door opened a crack. Shirley, the makeup girl, peered out.

Neil hadn't thought of what to say, but now that he was faced with her, his mind worked fast. "Hello," he said. "I've got a message for Harry Jenkins. He is here, isn't he?"

Shirley looked terrified. She said, "I don't know what you're talking about!" and shut the door firmly.

Neil stepped back and scanned the trailer. He was sure that Jenkins and Prince were there, but he couldn't see anything through the blinds that covered the windows. Slowly, he walked back to his friends.

"We've got to get in there somehow," said Penny.

"But if we try anything, he'll kill Prince," Max protested.

"No, I don't think he will," said Neil. "I don't think he would hurt a dog, no matter what he says. If we —"

Princess interrupted him. She was still tugging at her leash, and now she burst out into another flurry of excited barking.

"Good girl!" said Neil. "You can smell your dad, can't you?"

Before he had finished speaking, an answering bark came from the trailer.

"Prince!" Max exclaimed. "That's Prince!"

"All right!" said Neil.

"Listen, Max." Penny was speaking quickly. "We've got to tell the police now. We know he's got a stolen dog in there. I know the sergeant at Beckthwaite. He won't do anything careless. I'm going to phone."

Taking King with her, she headed back toward the castle. Max watched her go, and then stooped to pick up Princess, who was still barking furiously. He hugged her to him. "It'll be OK," he promised. Neil thought he was trying to convince himself.

He took a few steps out into the clearing. Raising his voice, he called, "Mr. Jenkins! We know you're in there. Bring Prince out now and you'll save yourself a lot of trouble."

Emily whispered behind him, "Don't mention the police." Neil nodded. There was no answer from the trailer except for more barking from Prince. The noise set Jake off as well, and Fred added a deep woof, too.

Neil had to calm Jake down before he could make himself heard again. "Mr. Jenkins! Let Prince come out. You're only —"

The door of the trailer opened. Harry Jenkins appeared, with Prince on a leash.

"Prince!" Max called. "Here, Prince!"

Prince pulled toward him to the full length of his leash, barking louder than ever. Harry Jenkins hesitated, as if he might decide to hand the cocker spaniel over, and then wrenched on the leash and dragged Prince away. Prince was still barking, trying to resist and go to Max, skidding and slithering through the snow as Jenkins jerked on the leash.

Neil took off in pursuit. Harry Jenkins was floundering up the slope that led to the road, stumbling in unseen hollows and slipping backward as the snow gave way under his feet. Prince, still hanging back, managed to get his leash caught up in a bramble bush. As Jenkins stopped to unwind it, Neil hurled himself forward and grabbed him around the waist. Jenkins fell backward with Neil on top of him.

Prince tugged himself free and dashed off in a flurry of snow, back down the slope toward Max.

As he struggled to hang on to Harry Jenkins, Neil could hear wild barking from the dogs as the others forced their way through the snowy undergrowth. Jenkins threw Neil off, but before he could get to his feet Emily caught up and grabbed him, and Neil heard another voice shouting his name from lower down the hill.

He got a grip on Harry, and looked back to see Lord Ainsworth, Penny, and Maggie Brown hurrying toward them through the trees. At the bottom of the slope, Max was kneeling in the snow with Prince in his arms. Princess danced around them, yapping joyfully at the top of her tiny voice.

Harry fought to stand upright, but with both Neil and Emily hanging on to him, and both Fred and Jake standing by, he couldn't run. Panting, he faced Lord Ainsworth. "Get him off of me!"

"I think they're doing a splendid job." Lord Ainsworth's voice was cold. "Maybe you'd like to explain what you're doing with a stolen dog?"

Harry Jenkins opened his mouth, but nothing came out. He sagged in Neil's grasp.

Neil called to Max, "Is he hurt, Max?"

Max was carefully looking over Prince. "No, I think he's fine."

"I wouldn't have hurt him," Jenkins protested. "I'd have given him back."

Lord Ainsworth snorted in disbelief. "Maybe. In any case, you can explain all that to the police."

As he spoke, there was the sound of a car engine. A police car slowly nosed its way down the track that led to the clearing, and parked beside the trailer. A police sergeant got out of it. Lord Ainsworth grabbed Harry's shoulder and propelled him back toward the car.

Neil and Emily followed. Beside the trailer, the makeup girl was sitting on a fallen log, crying quietly.

"Shirley, what are you doing mixed up in all this?" Maggie asked.

Shirley looked up at her. "He's my brother," she said. "I didn't want anything to do with it. And I didn't know he was going to steal the dog."

"That's right, she didn't," Jenkins said. "She let me sleep in the makeup van and made me up — but that's all."

"I'm sorry, miss," the police sergeant said, "but you'll have to come with us and make a statement."

Shirley got up, wiping her face with a handkerchief. "It's all gone wrong," she said. "And now I'll lose my job as well."

"I'll talk to Jeff," Maggie promised, but as Shirley got into the police car she didn't look as if she thought that would do much good.

Harry Jenkins glanced back to where Max was still crouching beside Prince. Princess was touching noses with her dad. Harry opened his mouth to say something, but as Max caught his eye he looked away and got into the car in silence. The sergeant drove off. Neil watched the car edge its way back up the track, wheels spinning to get a grip on the snow as it vanished among the trees.

"Let's hope that's the last of him," he said with satisfaction.

"Yes," said Penny, "and now we can get on with the film."

"There's only one problem," said Maggie. "Tomorrow's Christmas Eve. Jeff told me this morning that we can't possibly finish filming before Christmas. If we have to take down the sets and then come back afterward, it's going to cost a fortune."

"You mean the film might still be ruined?" Max asked, dismayed.

Neil and Emily looked at each other. They couldn't believe that, after all their efforts, Harry Jenkins might have done what he set out to do.

"Just a minute," said Lord Ainsworth. "What's all this about taking down the sets? Is there any reason why you can't stay here and finish?"

"But it's Christmas," said Maggie. "Surely you don't want the castle full of film people over Christmas?"

Lord Ainsworth's face, reddened from the cold, broke into a beaming smile. "Why not?"

Maggie gaped at him. "Why not . . . well . . ."

"You'll all be very welcome. Max, your parents are on their way already — they'll be welcome to stay, too. We'll all have a real medieval Christmas in Ainsworth Castle!"

Neil thought it was a great idea. The only problem was, he and Emily were due to go home. He was trying not to feel too disappointed when Penny came and grabbed his arm.

"Dad, we can invite Neil and Emily's mom and dad, can't we? And their little sister?"

"What?" Lord Ainsworth peered down at Neil and Emily. "Yes, of course we can. Let them all come!"

Lord Ainsworth got to his feet and rapped on the table for silence. As he waited, Neil looked around the Great Hall of Ainsworth Castle. Snow was swirling past the windows, but inside logs blazed up in the enormous fireplace. Bright lights shined on the Arthurian weapons and tapestries, and on the tables set for a magnificent Christmas dinner.

Penny had suggested using the Round Table for the Christmas feast, but the props master had re-

fused to risk damaging it, so long tables had been set up in a huge square, covered with white linen cloths, and topped with red candles in holders made from holly and pine cones. Silver cutlery and crystal glasses sparkled at each place setting.

Verity the wardrobe woman had surpassed herself to find costumes for everyone. Neil wore a blue velvet tunic instead of his peasant outfit, and both Emily and Penny wore long dresses. Penny's brother Rick, just home from music college, was dressed as a medieval minstrel. Even the guests were in costume. Neil thought the long, trailing gown of red velvet really suited Carole, his mom, though Bob Parker, his dad, looked a bit uncomfortable in a knight's heavy robes. Five-year-old Sarah, dressed as one of Morgan le Fay's imps, had hardly been able to stop twirling around to admire herself, and was wriggling excitedly in her chair.

It wasn't often that Bob and Carole left King Street Kennels, but Carole had told Neil that, with help from Kate and Bev, the kennel assistants, they'd arranged to stay at the castle overnight and go home the next day.

King and Fred were sprawled in front of the fire, just like the hounds in a real medieval hall, but Jake sat beside Neil's chair, and Prince beside Max. Neil wasn't sure where Princess had gotten off to. He'd been about to ask Max when Lord Ainsworth called for silence.

Gradually, everyone quieted down. Neil grinned across the table at Max and his parents, Fred's owner Bill Grey, and the rest of the actors and film crew who were sitting nearby. Everyone looked happy except Brett Benson. Maggie had told Neil that he was sulking because he'd planned to jet off to the Bahamas for Christmas and had to cancel his trip because of the filming. *Serves him right,* Neil thought.

The only member of the film crew who wasn't there was Shirley. Jeff Calton had pulled her off the film, but Maggie had persuaded him not to fire her. She had gone home for Christmas with her brother Harry, who was out on bail until his case came up for trial. No one knew what his sentence would be, but one thing was certain: his career with dogs was finished. Neil thought there couldn't be a worse punishment.

"Before we start to eat," Lord Ainsworth began, "I'd like to say a few words. First, welcome, all of you, to Ainsworth Castle. It must be hundreds of years since a Lord Ainsworth sat down to eat with such splendid company."

So let's get on with it, Neil pleaded silently. *I'm starving!*

"I'd also like to wish you a very happy Christmas, and, to our friends from Prince Productions, a successful conclusion to your filming. I'm sure we're all glad to hear that Prince is safe and well, and I, for one, am looking forward to seeing Ainsworth Castle on the screen as Camelot."

Scratching his moustache and smiling a little, he went on. "One of you film people told me that it was King Arthur's custom never to sit down to a feast until he'd heard a piece of wonderful news. I think we ought to stick to these old customs, and so I've got some news I'd like to share with you. Adrian . . . ?"

"What's all this about?" Neil asked Emily.

Emily just shrugged, but Penny's eyes were sparkling, as if she knew something they didn't.

Adrian had turned scarlet, and he looked embarrassed as he got to his feet and cleared his throat. "Er . . . yes . . . well, I'm delighted to announce that Verity, who some of you know is the wardrobe person for Prince Productions, and as you can all see is doing a marvelous job . . ." He paused, and gave up the tangled sentence. "I asked Verity to marry me, and she said yes."

Applause broke out all around the table. Verity blushed pink and smiled.

Neil nearly choked into his drink. "*That's* why he was lurking up in the Long Gallery!"

"And why he looked so flustered," said Emily. "I bet Brett Benson caught him kissing Verity!"

Lord Ainsworth took over again. "So Verity will be leaving Prince Productions, but she's going to set up a display of costumes here at Ainsworth Castle, for the visitors who come to see where the film was made. And I'm sure we all hope that she and Adrian will be very happy. Will you all drink a toast, please, to Adrian and Verity."

Everyone rose to their feet and raised their glasses. "To Adrian and Verity!"

Waiters came in from one end of the hall with roasted turkeys on huge silver platters, dishes of vegetables, sauces and gravy boats. Neil didn't know if it was what King Arthur would have eaten, but it looked good to him.

As he took his seat again, he could hardly believe that all their troubles were over. Prince was back safely with Max, and in the next few days the film would be finished. Meanwhile, they could all look forward to a real Arthurian Christmas.

No, he corrected himself, *a real doggy Christmas.* Because Christmas wouldn't be the same without dogs to share it. He felt a sudden pang of unhappiness that Jake's dad Sam wasn't with him anymore, but he knew that the best thing he could do for Sam's memory was to give everything he could to the dogs who were here.

But where's Princess? he wondered again.

As the thought crossed his mind, he heard a high-pitched yap from across the table. Princess poked her head up from where she was sitting on Max's lap, and put both forepaws on the white cloth, as if she was waiting to be served.

"Max . . ." his mother said, laughing.

Max looked apologetic. "Well, it is Christmas. And she tracked Prince down. We wouldn't be enjoying this now if it wasn't for Princess. She did it all!"

"She sure did," said Neil. "If anybody deserves a Christmas dinner, it's Princess. She's a real star!"